First published in Belgium and Holland by Clavis Uitgeverij, Hasselt – Amsterdam, 2012
Copyright © 2012, Clavis Uitgeverij

English translation from the Dutch by Clavis Publishing Inc. New York
Copyright © 2013 for the English language edition: Clavis Publishing Inc. New York

Visit us on the web at www.clavisbooks.com

My Baby Book. Hooray, I Am a Girl! written and illustrated by Liesbet Slegers
Original title: *Joepie, ik ben een meisje!*
Translated from the Dutch by Clavis Publishing

ISBN 978-1-60537-145-0

This book was printed in January 2013 at Proost, Everdongenlaan 23, 2300 Turnhout, Belgium

First Edition
10 9 8 7 6 5 4 3 2 1

Hooray, I Am a Girl!

Liesbet Slegers

Clavis

NEW YORK

First I am in Mommy's tummy.

Then I am born!

When I am one month old, I can already smile.

I get lots of hugs and hear lots of words.

Everyone is so curious about me!

I didn't like eating with a spoon
for the first time.

And then... it's my first birthday party!

I get to wear a crown on my head
and I get nice presents.

Come and see how this all happened!

In the tummy

I am here,
but you can't see me,
warm inside Mommy's tummy.
She sings me a lullaby.
I tickle and kick.
I tumble and turn.
Here is my little foot—hop!

I've just arrived in Mommy's tummy and everyone is already talking about me!

When my daddy heard that I was inside
Mommy's tummy, he said/did this:

....

When my mommy heard that I was inside her tummy, she said/did this:

....

When did Mommy and Daddy tell the good news
to their family, friends, and colleagues?

....

When did Mommy and Daddy buy me my first clothes?

....

They bought ....

What did Mommy and Daddy think I was? boy/girl
When was my due date to be born?

....

PICTURE of
Mommy's big
tummy

This is Mommy's big tummy.

I am inside. It is nice and warm in there.

I can hear Mommy's heart beating. It makes me calm.

Just a little more patience, I'll be here for a while...

Mommy is getting everything ready.

This is an ultrasound scan of me.
Now Mommy and Daddy can see me
inside Mommy's tummy,
but I am well hidden.
How exciting!

ULTRASOUND SCAN
at ... weeks

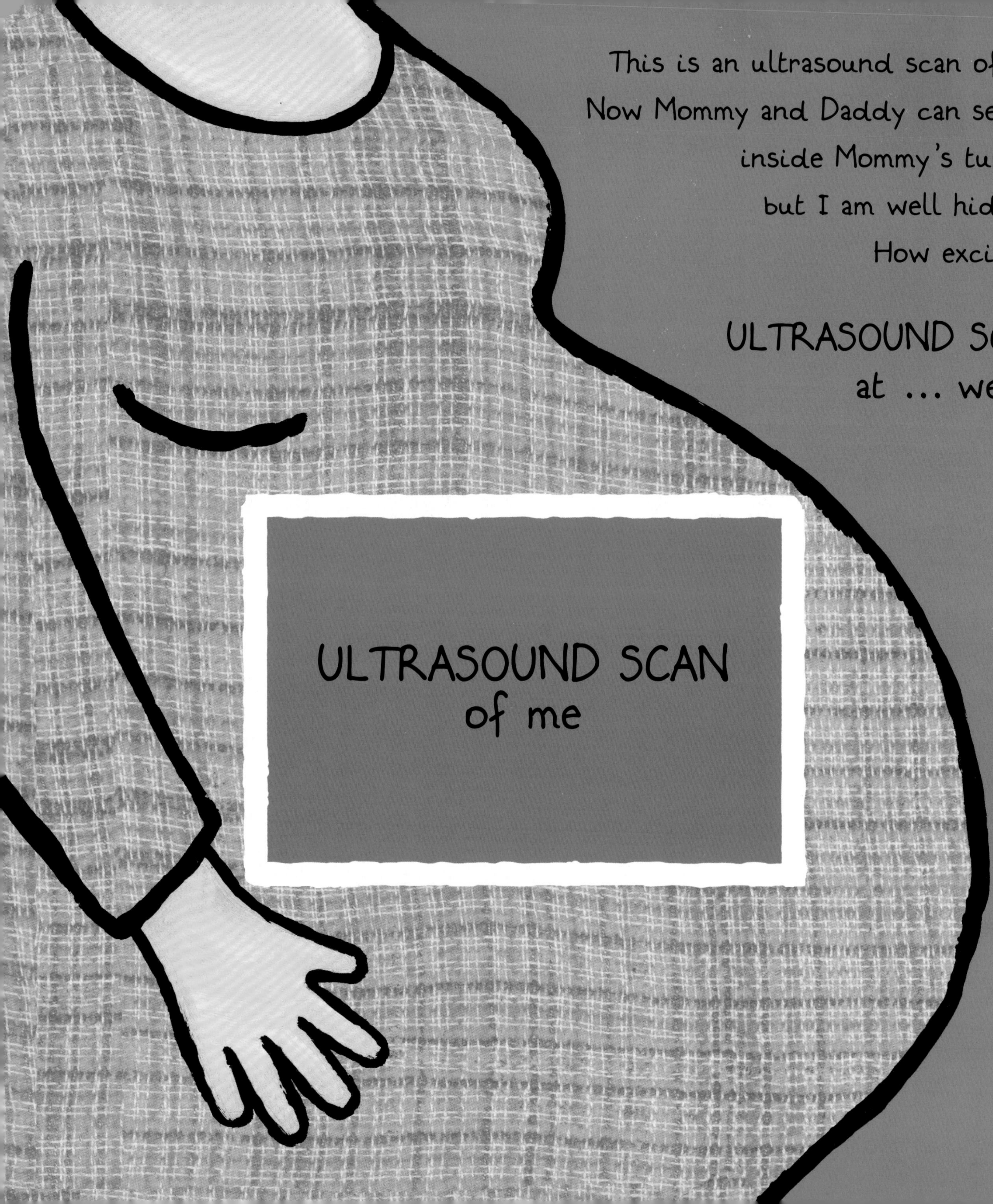

ULTRASOUND SCAN
of me

Inside Mommy's tummy I hear lots of noises. I love it when Mommy and Daddy try to tell me things! When I like something, I kick my feet.

Some noises I can hear:

Talking

Soft music

Singing

and..

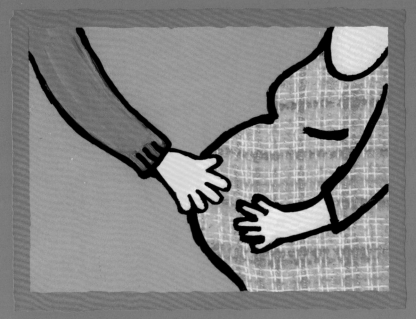

Stroking Mommy's tummy

The doctor can hear my tiny heart beating. Yes, it's really me! I love to kick and turn around, and after a while, I can even open my eyes. But most of the time, I am asleep. I get lots of food through the umbilical cord. And I like to suck my little thumb!

Here is an ultrasound scan of me at ... weeks:

I get tiny hairs all over my body and my head. My fingers and toes are growing every day. Everything is growing and I'm getting bigger and bigger. Just a bit longer and then I'll be born!

ULTRASOUND SCAN of me

My mommy's doctor can see how big I am and how much I weigh:

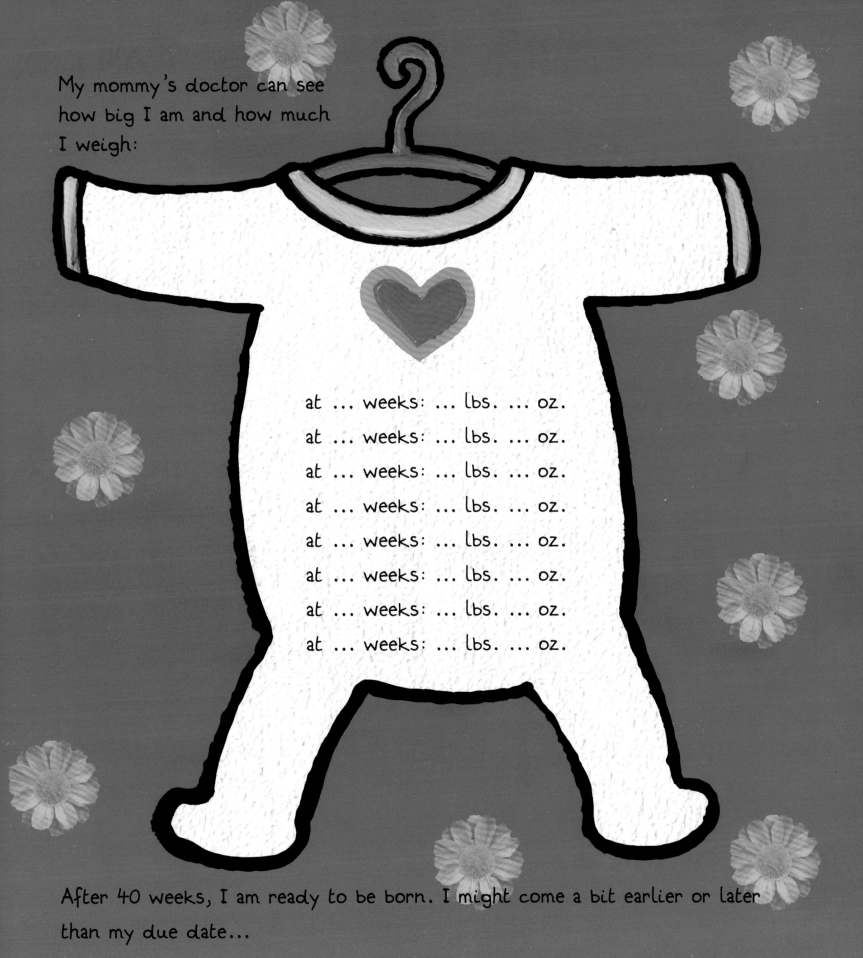

at ... weeks: ... lbs. ... oz.
at ... weeks: ... lbs. ... oz.
at ... weeks: ... lbs. ... oz.
at ... weeks: ... lbs. ... oz.
at ... weeks: ... lbs. ... oz.
at ... weeks: ... lbs. ... oz.
at ... weeks: ... lbs. ... oz.
at ... weeks: ... lbs. ... oz.

After 40 weeks, I am ready to be born. I might come a bit earlier or later than my due date...

My birth

Hello, here I am!
I've made my trip into this world
from Mommy's tummy to Mommy and Daddy.
Hooray, I am a girl!

The day of my birth (that is my birthday!)

I am born and I am a **girl!**

My name is ....

Mommy and Daddy are so happy! Welcome, sweet girl!
We love you!

PICTURE of me
on the day I was born.

Here is my birth announcement:

I am born on

Time: ......

My weight: ....

My length: ....

My mommy's name:....................... My daddy's name:.......................

The doctor or
midwife's name:

....

The weather on my

birth day:

....

My astrological sign:

....

I am born in

 spring

 summer

 fall

 winter

My address:

....

....

Place of birth:

....

Room number: ....

This was in the news

on the day I was born:

....

....

This is the first thing I did when I was born:

O cry   O be quiet   O open my eyes   O keep my eyes closed

O ....

What Daddy did when I was born:

O cry

O laugh

O faint

O give me and Mommy kisses

O ....

What Mommy did when I was born:

O cry

O laugh

O give me and Daddy kisses

O ....

My first visitors
(in the hospital):

....

My first milk (from Mommy's
breast/from a bottle):

....

The first clothes I wore:

....

My first presents:

....

My first dress was a gift from

....

and it looked like this:

....

PICTURE of me,
I'm a few days
old here!

O I got to go home on

(date)

....

O I was born at home

Who lives with us (pets, too!)

....

My first day and night at home were like this:

....

My first month

Now I am at home.
I am so happy here:
Eating, sleeping, having a bath;
lying next to Mommy and Daddy;
getting lots of hugs and kisses every day!

After a few weeks, I look like this:

PICTURE of me
when I'm asleep

I'm asleep
Unforgettable moments:
....
....

PICTURE of me
when I'm awake

I'm awake

The first time I go on a trip:

....

....

How I am at home:

O   I keep Mommy and Daddy awake at night

O   I sleep a lot at night

O   I mix up day and night

O   I drink a lot

O   I don't drink a lot

O   I am pretty quiet

O   I like to make noise

O   ....

This is how I like to be comforted:

O   lying on Mommy or Daddy's tummy

O   rocked in Mommy or Daddy's arms

O   held against Mommy or Daddy's shoulder

O   lying in my crib

O   walking or driving in the car

O   ....

I'm still little and there are lots of things I can't do yet.
Mommy and Daddy take such good care of me!
I enjoy:

A splashy bath

A clean diaper

Warm milk

A quiet nap

My family

I love being with Mommy and Daddy;
sister and brother; Grandma and Grandpa.
They're all standing in line to give me
a big hug.

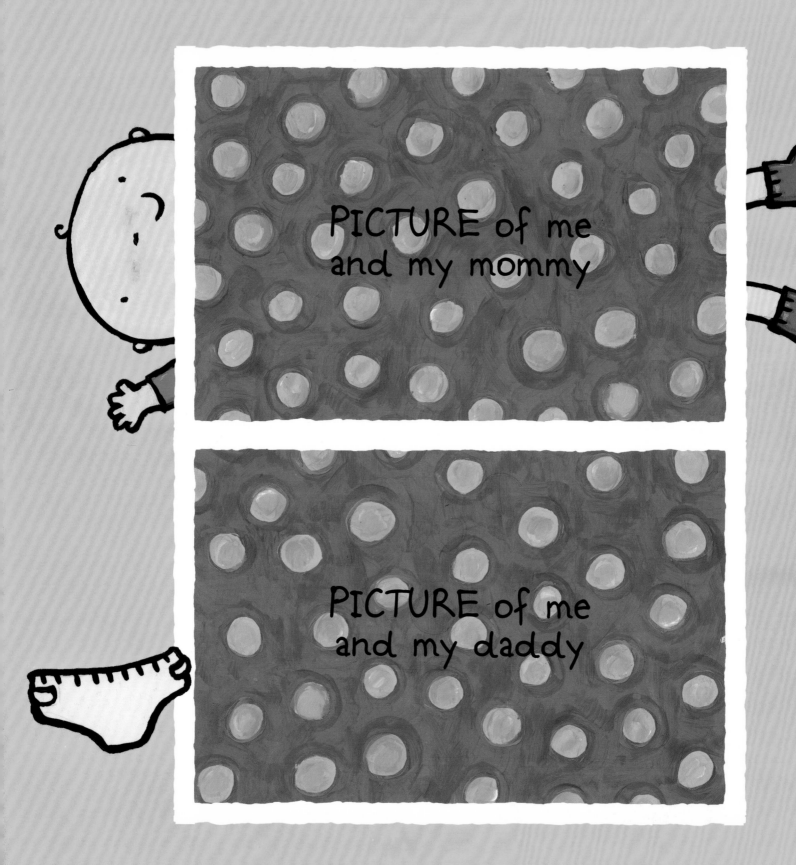

My family members dream of doing this with me when I am older:

Mommy:

....

Daddy:

....

Grandma and Grandpa:

....

....

Who else?

....

What do I love most?
check the box

My brother(s) name(s) is/are: ....

My sister(s) name(s) is/are: ....

O   I am the only child

My maternal grandparents' names are: ....

This is what I call them: ....

My paternal grandparents' names are: ....

This is what I call them: ....

PICTURE of me
and my family

Here are some pictures, notes,
and cards from when I was born...

The first time...

What can I do already?
I roll and I crawl.
I eat food from a spoon.
I babble and laugh.
I take my first steps!

The first time I was fed with a spoon!

That was on ....

I ate: strained vegetables / strained fruit

How was it? *check the box*

I liked it and
ate it all up

I didn't like it
and I cried

I was angry and pushed
the spoon away

PICTURE of my first
meal with a spoon

The first time I turned over by myself:

....

The first time I sat up by myself:

....

The first time I crawled:

....

My first steps:

....

My first tooth:

....

My first word was:

....

he first time I slept all through the night:

....

My first trip:

....

This is the first drawing I made with Mommy and Daddy's help:

My first book:

....

My first toy:

....

PICTURE: This is
how I play!

My first birthday

Hip, hip, hurray!
It's my birthday!
We eat cake!
I get presents
and cards!

On my birthday we celebrate the day I was born.
It's a party! The whole house is decorated.

PICTURE of me
on my first birthday

Who is at my first birthday party?

....

What presents do I get on my first birthday? ....

We eat ....

and drink ....

We sing ....

I can do this on my first birthday:

....

....

....

With whom do I play
on my first birthday?

....

....

....

 This is my first
birthday card!

 This is a piece of
wrapping paper from
my first present.

For she's a jolly good fellow.
For she's a jolly good fellow.
For she's a jolly good fellow
and so say all of us!

It's someone's birthday today,
hurray, hurray!
Yes, you can see that it's hers!
We all like this, oh yes,
and that's why we sing
Happy birthday, hurray, hurray!
(x 3)

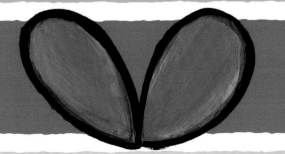

Oh, we're so happy today
it's ....'s birthday! (x 2)
Oh, we're so happy today
it's ....'s birthday!
And that's why we celebrate!

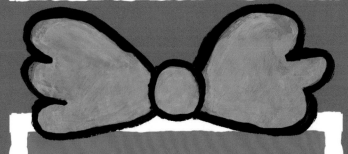

Happy birthday to you,
happy birthday to you!
Happy birthday, dear

....

Happy birthday to you!

Here are some pictures, notes,
and cards from my first birthday:

I am a big girl now!